Moonhorse

by Mary Pope Osborne

illustrated by

S. M. Saelig

THE BODLEY HEAD · LONDON

First published in 1991 by The Bodley Head Children's Books
an imprint of The Random Century Group Ltd
20 Vauxhall Bridge Road, London SW1V 2SA

Random Century Australia Pty Ltd
20 Alfred Street, Sydney, NSW 2061, Australia

Random Century New Zealand Ltd,
PO Box 40-086, Glenfield, Auckland 10, New Zealand

Random Century South Africa Pty Ltd
PO Box 337, Bergvlei 2012, South Africa

First published in the United States of America in 1991 by Alfred A. Knopf Inc

Printed and bound in the United States of America

British Library Cataloguing in Publication Data is available

ISBN 0 370 31601 0

To the memory of my father

M. P. O.

To Dorothy

S. M. S.

We rock on the porch,
my dad and I,
while a thin moon hides
behind the trees.

In the distance a whistle blows.
A flock of blackbirds
leaves the grass.

I see a star, first star tonight.
"Look, Dad," I say, "let's make a wish!"
But Daddy's quiet;
he's gone to sleep.

Now I feel lonely in the dark.
So I make a wish
by myself.

The wind blows,
and birds cry.

Out of the night
the Moonhorse appears.

I slip from Dad's lap
and run through the grass.
I touch the white horse
and whisper, "Hey, boy."
He nuzzles my cheek.

I grab his white mane
and climb on his back,

and we rise
through the night.

We fly over mountains,
through cloud-stuff and mist,

high over twilight,

'til we land on a star.

I water the Moonhorse,
brush dust from his eyes.
Together we lasso
the new moon below.

We pull very hard.
Then the Moonhorse and I
pull the Moon through the sky!

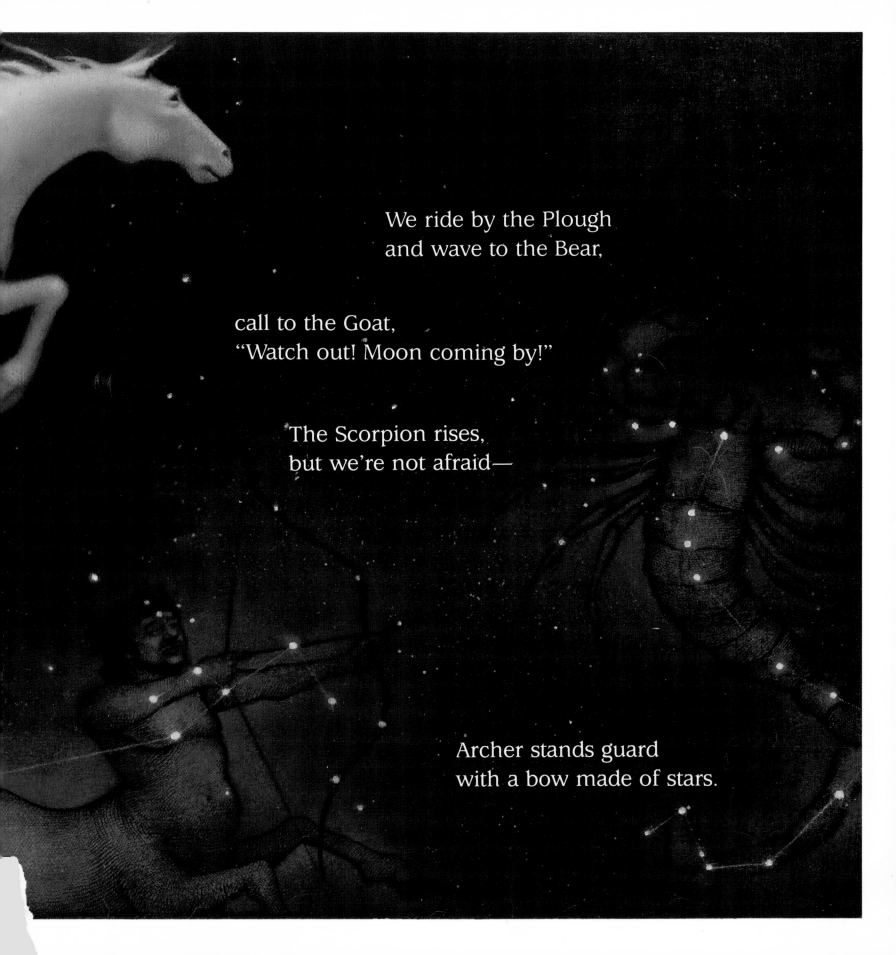

We ride by the Plough
and wave to the Bear,

call to the Goat,
"Watch out! Moon coming by!"

The Scorpion rises,
but we're not afraid—

Archer stands guard
with a bow made of stars.

Wolf shadows chase us!
"Fly, Moonhorse, fly!"

Then a comet shoots past,
and we leap, lose the wolves
in a shower of light.

We gallop towards midnight,
the Moonhorse and I,
pulling the Moon
through the clear southern sky,

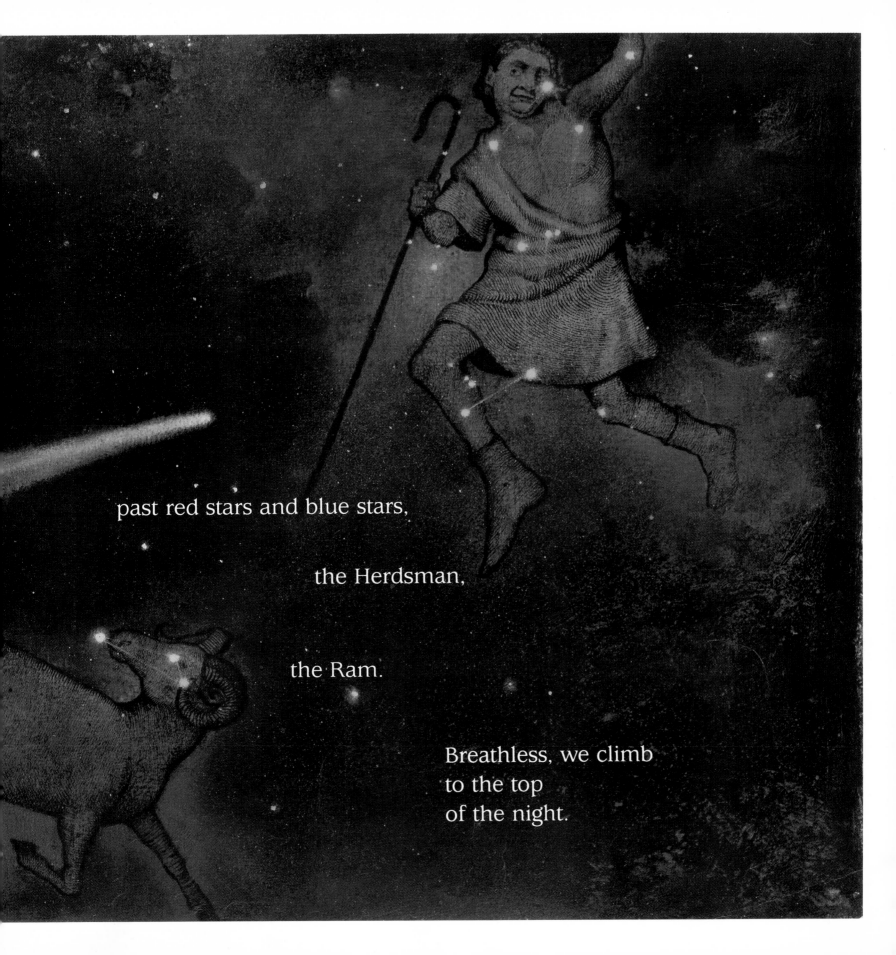

past red stars and blue stars,

the Herdsman,

the Ram.

Breathless, we climb
to the top
of the night.

Then I tell the new moon,
"We have to go now.
You can drift on your own
down to the dawn.
You're safe from the shadows
and the Scorpion, too."

The Moonhorse and I say
good night to our Moon,
let go of our rope
and glide back to earth.

We float through the darkness,
through stardust and clouds,

down through the sky,
'til we land in our yard.

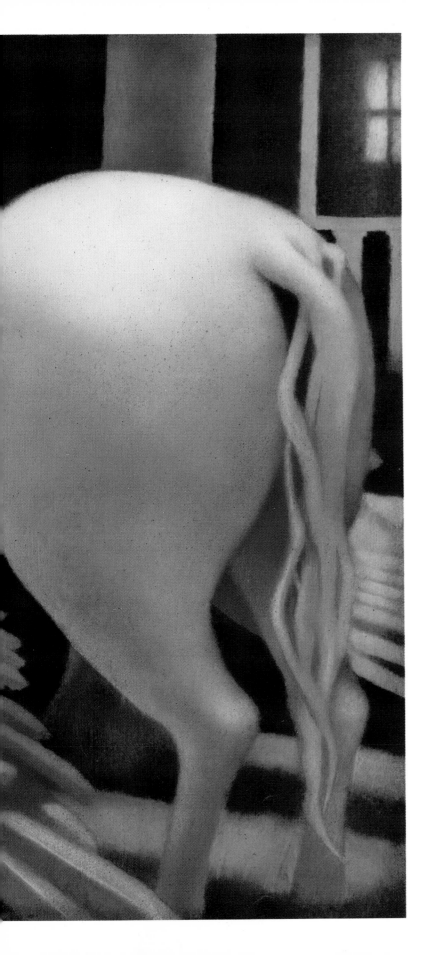

I hug the Moonhorse,
say gently,
"Sorry to go,
but I need my dad now."

He stands by the trees
'til I'm safe on the porch.

Daddy's still sleeping,
so I tap on his head
and whisper, "Wake up.
You rocked off to sleep."

"Goodness," he says,
"the Moon's high in the sky."
"I know it. We helped her,
the Moonhorse and I."

Wind starts to blow,
and birds start to cry.

Swish, swish . . .
"What's that?" Daddy says.

"Wings, Dad.
Wave good-bye."